Make the Best of It

By Christine Economos
Illustrated by Janice Skivington

Copyright © 2000 Metropolitan Teaching and Learning Company.
Published by Metropolitan Teaching and Learning Company.
Printed in the United States of America.
ISBN 1-58120-043-9

3 4 5 6 7 8 9 CL 03 02 01

"I have a surprise for you, Jed," said Dad. "We're going on a camping trip. We'll spend two nights by the lake. It will be an adventure. You can come with us if you like, Dan."

"A camping trip! What fun!" said Jed.

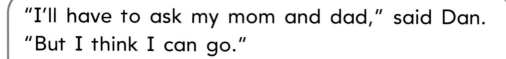

"I'll have to ask my mom and dad," said Dan. "But I think I can go."

"You'll need to pack bags," said Dad. "Just pack what you'll need for two nights. We'll have a lot of fun."

3

"What an adventure," said Dan. "We'll look for gold. At night, we'll cook over a fire."

"I bet we do find gold by the lake," said Jed.

"I don't think we'll find much gold," said Dad. "We'll find a lot of trees and bugs."

4

"I found a good spot for a camp," said Dad. "We can put the tent up over by that tree."

"Here is the tent," said Jed. "Boy. This tent is old! Look. I found a little rip!"

"I found some rips, too," said Dan.

5

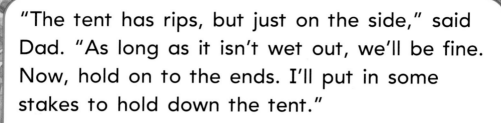

"The tent has rips, but just on the side," said Dad. "As long as it isn't wet out, we'll be fine. Now, hold on to the ends. I'll put in some stakes to hold down the tent."

"Do we need another stake here?" asked Jed.

"We don't have any more. If we have all of the stakes but one, the tent will stand up," said Dad. "We're camping. We have to make the best of it. Now I'll get a fire going. Jed, you find a log. You can look, too, Dan."

7

"Here are two old logs," said Jed. "Can we use them to make the fire?"

"They'll work," said Dad. "You and Dan bring the food. It is in the bag by that big tree. We'll have a nice fire in no time."

"The logs are too damp. I can't make a fire with them," said Dad. "I hope I can find one that isn't damp. It is very wet and cold here."

"We may not need a fire," said Jed. "Don't laugh, but we can't find the food."

9

"It looks like I didn't bring all the food," said Dad. "Here are hot dog buns and some jam. They'll do for now."

"It is a damp, cold night," said Jed. "We have a tent with rips, no fire, and no hot food. What a laugh!"

"You two said you wanted to camp. You said you wanted an adventure," said Dad. "This is an adventure. We can make the best of it!"

"You're right, Dad," said Jed. "I'll get the lamp. We need to see what we're eating."

11

"I didn't think camping would be like this," said Dan. "I didn't think I would be so cold."

"Or so damp," said Jed. "Dad, are you up yet? We have to go to the lake. It is time for our big adventure."

12

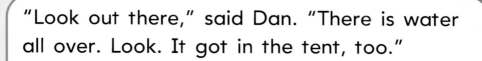

"Look out there," said Dan. "There is water all over. Look. It got in the tent, too."

"Did you bring books?" asked Dad. "We can read by the lamp for a little bit. Then it will let up. You'll see."

"Jed has a map. I can read this joke book," said Dan. "It will make me laugh."

"Hold it. I found a place on the map," said Jed. "We can eat there. We can make the best of it, Dad. We can eat out. How about it?"

"I could go for some hot cakes," said Dad.

"Hot cakes!" said Jed. "They'll hit the spot. Dan, get the lamp. We'll pack up the camp."

"So long, big adventure. And so long, old tent," said Dan. "Hot cakes, here I come!"

"What a camping trip!" said Dad. "We had a tent with rips, no fire, and cold food. But we made the best of it. What an adventure! What did you like best, boys?"

"The hot cakes!" said Jed and Dan.